Copyright © 2024 by Savannah Posley and Posley GLOBAL, LLC

All rights reserved. No part of this publication may be reproduced, distributed, or transmitted in any form or by any means, including photocopying, recording, or other electronic or mechanical methods, without the prior written permission of the publisher, except in the case of brief quotations embodied in critical reviews and certain other noncommercial uses permitted by copyright law.

BZZZ!!! (The Ice Cream Crime)

Written by Savannah Posley
Illustrated by Vladimir Cebu
Published by Posley GLOBAL, LLC
Typesetting by Ridwan Amaludin

First Edition: June 2024

Published in Glenwood, Illinois

ISBN: 978-1-963449-00-6

This book is a work of fiction. Names, characters, places, and incidents either are the product of the author's imagination or are used fictitiously. Any resemblance to actual persons, living or dead, events, or locales is entirely coincidental.

Printed in USA

Posley GLOBAL, LLC
Library of Congress Control Number: 2024911187
www.expectingmountains.com

For inquiries regarding permissions, please contact:

Permissions Department

Posley GLOBAL, LLC
19 West Main Street
Glenwood, IL
60425-9998
P.O. Box 20
Email: www.95Notes@gmail.com

Cover design by Youness El Hindami
Interior design by Vlamir Cebu
Typeset by Ridwan Amaludin

Disclaimer: The characters and events depicted in this book, "Bzzz!!! The Ice Cream Crime," are purely fictional. Any resemblance to actual persons, living or dead, or to actual events is purely coincidental. The author and publisher do not condone or promote any form of violence or harmful actions. The story is intended for entertainment purposes only and should not be taken as a reflection of real-life situations. Readers are encouraged to use their imagination and enjoy the whimsical journey of Brianna and Flernado's friendship.

We hope you enjoy reading BZZZ!!! (The Ice Cream Crime) as much as we enjoyed creating it! Thank you for supporting children's literature.

Cover and interior illustrations © 2023 Youness El Hindami and Vladimir Cebu

My Enemy

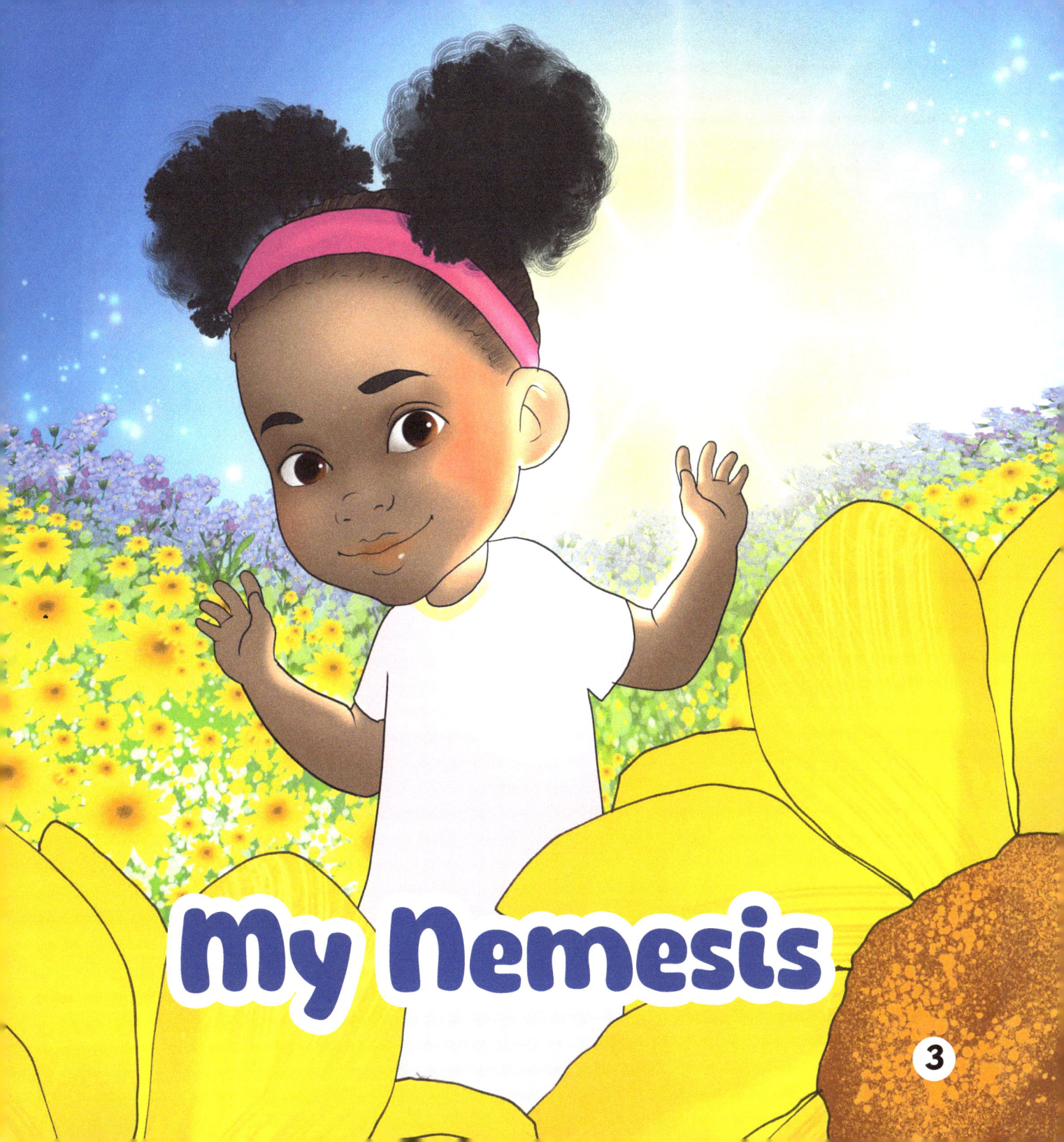

While I was gone, my mommy got me the grandest, greatest, yummiest, most delicious thing ever!

Today's ICE CREAM was not just your regular everyday old boring ice cream. My own mommy picked up my most favorite, delish dessert of them all.

Today, my mommy bought me not one but two scoops of Rainbow Sweet Delight's So Wonderful Ice Cream, topped with a cloud of mouthwatering whipped cream and finally finished off with picture-perfect ruby red cherries. This masterpiece was a creation right out of a cartoon.

Just as my extra special ice cream spoon was about to dive deep into this creamy rainbow sweet delight display of deliciousness, it appeared.

A foul and filthy fly flew its feet into the grandest,
greatest, yummiest, most delicious,
and most delightful treat ever created.

The fly dodged each and every one of my attacks like an evasive African antelope running from a hungry African lion.

I imagined this icky fly licking its yucky lips and thinking about my sweet, delicious, and delightful rainbow-flavored ice cream.

So, I ran full speed, looking to take the fly out with my final knockout fly swatter knuckle punch.

But in my haste and mad taste, I tripped and slipped on one of my stinky yellow socks that also played the role of its evil cousin, the banana peel. Mommy was right, "I should have cleaned up my dirty room!" I yelled as I fell to the ground.

As I fell, the fly-swatting secret weapon that I gripped tight like a rope swam away from my hand like a jellyfish jiggling in the ocean.

I landed heavy and hard on the floor. My head was a cool mint milkshake as it bounced around on the carpet.

Now both dazed and confused, the fly and I laid side by side, stuck and staring into each other's stars as they danced about over the top of each of our heads.

Up close, Brianna noticed that the fly was not so icky. Brianna was close enough to see his glasses which were kind of cool.

"Well, why didn't you just ask?" The girl quickly questioned the ice cream criminal like a superstar detective.

The fly turned its back, cried, and replied, "Most people don't like me. Most people hate it when I come around. They tell me to fly my filthy foul fly self away."

Brianna's eyes thawed. "Fly, we can be friends, but you have to ask if you want something. You can't just go around taking stuff. You can't just go around putting your filthy feet into someone else's favorite ice cream snack."

"BZZZ!!

Yes, I can agree to that if you can agree to use your words first instead of using those fists of fury," the fly said.

"Yes, I will promise as long as you also promise. I am sorry for not using my words. Do we have a deal?" Brianna asked the fly.

"BZZZ! Deal!"

The fly buzzed in response as they both shook hands.

"So, what is your name?" Brianna asked her newest fly friend.

"My name is Brianna.
It is so nice to officially meet you."

"So, would you like some ice cream, Flernado? Luckily, my mom bought two cups! You can have this one," Brianna said to the fly.

Brianna's Favorite Ice Cream Cone Craft with Optional Toppings:

Let's create Brianna's Favorite Ice Cream Cone Craft with Optional Toppings inspired by the story "Bzzz!!! The Ice Cream Crime"!

Materials needed:

- Construction paper (various colors)
- Scissors
- Glue
- Markers or crayons
- Popsicle sticks
- Pom-poms or cotton balls
- Googly eyes (optional)
- Sequins, glitter, or stickers (optional)

Instructions:

1. Cut out a large triangle shape from brown construction paper to represent the ice cream cone, just like the cone Flernado landed on.
2. Cut out smaller triangles from different colored construction paper to represent different flavors of ice cream, just like the rainbow ice cream in the story.
3. Glue the smaller triangles onto the larger triangle to create the ice cream scoops on top of the cone, just like the ice cream cone Brianna was eating.
4. Decorate the ice cream scoops with markers or crayons to make them look delicious and colorful, just like the vibrant ice cream in the story.
5. Optionally, add sequins, glitter, or stickers to the ice cream scoops for a sparkly and festive look, just like the decorations at the ice cream shop.
6. Glue pom-poms or cotton balls onto the top of each ice cream scoop to represent whipped cream, just like the whipped cream on Brianna's ice cream.
7. Optionally, add googly eyes to the pom-poms or cotton balls for a fun and silly appearance, just like the funny faces Brianna made with whipped cream.
8. Allow the glue to dry completely.

9. Once dry, flip the ice cream cone over and glue a popsicle stick to the back to create a handle, just like the handle Flernado used to take the ice cream cone.
10. Let the craft project dry completely.
11. Once dry, your child can use their ice cream cone craft as a decoration or even as a puppet to reenact scenes from the book, just like Brianna and Flernado did.

Remember to supervise children during the craft activity and assist them with cutting or gluing as needed. Feel free to get creative with additional toppings and decorations. Enjoy making Brianna's favorite ice cream cone craft with optional toppings, just like in the story "Bzzz!!! The Ice Cream Crime"!

Reflection Questions for BZZZ! The Ice Cream Crime

Directions: Answer the following reflection questions based on the story. Responses should be thoughtful.

1. Identify the characters in the story.
   _____
   _____

2. Describe the setting of the ice cream story.
   _____
   _____

3. What conflict or problem does Brianna encounter in the story?
   _____
   _____

4. Explain how Brianna overcomes her obstacles in the story.
   _____
   _____

5. Share a personal experience where you had to overcome a challenge. Describe what happened and what you did to overcome your problem.
   _____
   _____

Personal Connection Questions for BZZZ! The Ice Cream Crime

Directions: Answer the following personal connection questions based on the story. Responses should be thoughtful.

1. What are your top three favorite foods?
   _____
   _____

2. Which page in the book is your favorite? Describe the possible message conveyed by the illustration.
   _____
   _____

3. Why do you think the author chose the title "BZZZ! The Ice Cream Crime"?
   _____
   _____

4. If you could ask the author a question, what would it be?
   _____
   _____

5. Summarize the book in two or three sentences.
   _____
   _____

Welcome to the BZZZ!!! (The Ice Cream Crime) Word Search activity, inspired by the exciting children's book written by Savannah Posley. In this word search, you will be searching for ten words that are related to the story. These words can be hidden horizontally, vertically, diagonally, or even backward within the puzzle grid. However, remember that the words will never overlap or intersect with each other. Take a moment to familiarize yourself with the ten words listed below:

Nemesis, Grandest, Prototype, Deliciousness, Antelope, Evasive, Frantically, Empathy, Caring, BZZZ

Whenever you find a word, circle or highlight it to mark it as found. This will help you keep track of the words you've already discovered. Once you've completed the word search, double-check your work to make sure you haven't missed any words. After you finish, feel free to share your favorite word that you found and why it is significant to the book BZZZ!!! (The Ice Cream Crime). Remember, this worksheet is a bonus activity that accompanies the book BZZZ!!! (The Ice Cream Crime). Enjoy the adventure and happy word searching!

```
S Q B A S F W H Y X Y M T M X B S F G B
M K S L L S J U Y Q B M D Q G S C L G B
M J I X O R E Z Y Z X N M U E B M P N D
U V S K U M Y V A L E F Z N O S W A I R
H P M D L U E I G Q L G S U Z E W X R P
Z S E Q S E P Q X G Y U G B Z Z Z P A I
X I Z Z K I L Q S A O I U C D W P J C Q
P H Z O V G L V S I S E M E N O G Y J Y
O I R H O C U Q C M T M I V P Y V G H Y
X A O K L R G I J H U O F I G J S T G L
E J O D D E L O E E X W S S F N A M A L
P E F C I E X C E B X C H A R P O I M A
O H Z G D O S Y S Y J F C V M E V I W C
L N I R G B A G J H B E Q E Z E Q Y E I
E Y D A J W G B F R W J X U F R Q N Z T
T F Z N J X Z R B L E I Q R L E Y H V N
N S E D J W Y M P P A E V E K O P V C F A
A C W E T O M R P R O T O T Y P E F W R
I K L S F U H A E V P T S X A O M D M F
P W C T I X H Z B L H J V F C Y Z R V E
```

Printed in the USA
CPSIA information can be obtained
at www.ICGtesting.com
LVHW071724110724
785088LV00016B/4